SL-90

1st

FROM ME TO YOU

Paul Rogers

Pictures by Jane Johnson

ORCHARD BOOKS
A division of Franklin Watts, Inc.
New York & London

For my mother

ORCHARD BOOKS
387 Park Avenue South, New York, New York 10016

Orchard Books Great Britain
10 Golden Square, London W1R 3AF, England

Orchard Books Canada
20 Torbay Road, Markham, Ontario 23P 1G6

Orchard Books is a division of Franklin Watts, Inc.

Manufactured in Belgium
Book design by Jennifer Campbell
The text in this book is set in 18pt. Caslon 540.
The illustrations are pen and ink drawings with watercolor.

10 9 8 7 6 5 4 3 2 1

Library of Congress Cataloging-in-Publication Data

Rogers, Paul, 1950 –
    From me to you.

    Summary: A grandmother shares her memories of three
generations with a young granddaughter and presents her
with a precious gift.
    [1. Grandmothers — Fiction.   2. Stories in rhyme]
I. Johnson, Jane, 1951–   ill. II. Title.
PZ8.3.R645Fr 1987 [E] 87-7943
ISBN 0-531-05732-1
ISBN 0-531-08332-2 (lib. bdg.)

I came headfirst into this world
eighty years ago.
Inside, gas lamps and firelight,
outside was white with snow.

Or so my mother told me.
What does a baby know?

Two brothers and a sister:
Harry, James and Tess.
And who's that in the christening robe —
that baby — can you guess?
My grandma sewed the lace by hand
on the little dress.

We had some fun, the four of us.
We once tossed a mud pie
in Mrs. Morgan's pantaloons
hanging up to dry.

And father spanked us one by one.
And I saw Harry cry.

James became a carpenter.   Harry went to sea.

And Tess became a lady and had us all to tea.

Alone at night, I used to dream
what might become of me.

I fell in love with Grandad.

My mother found that lace.

She pinned it on my wedding dress, then stitched it into place.

When Grandad turned to me in church,
you should have seen his face!

At last we had a little girl,
born one summer's day.
With that same lace I trimmed the crib
where your mother lay.

She was asleep beneath a tree when Grandad went away.

And now I'm getting very old.
Some things are hard to do —
like climb this hill! But I can still
stitch a thing or two.

Look what I've made with what was left.

Do you like it? It's for you.

FROM ME TO YOU is one Grandmother's story. This Grandmother was born in 1906. Her family was an ordinary, middle-class family, not poor and not rich. The small town they lived in was lit with gas light. They did not have electricity there yet. The rooms of their house were heated with coal fires. There was no central heating in the house and no plumbing except for cold running water in the kitchen. Water for baths was heated on the coal stove in the kitchen. People washed in wash basins and in tubs they filled by hand. Most clothes, especially clothes for children, were sewn at home. Boys wore big hats and short pants until they were about twelve. Little girls always wore dresses, never overalls, even when they went outdoors to play.

As is true in many large families, Grandma's brothers and sisters grew up to have lives quite different from their parents and from each other. Her brother James worked as a carpenter, building houses. Harry went to sea as a ship's officer on an ocean-going liner, a large boat that carried passengers back and forth across the Atlantic. Tess married a man who was rich and well-known, but she didn't become too proud to love her brothers and sisters. Grandma was the youngest. She dreamed about what her future might hold because, while some women worked in the 1920's when she was a girl, they were not considered to be suitable for many jobs and professions. Grandma married Grandad, and, like many women before her, she settled down to keep house.

At last, in the late 1930's, Grandma's and Grandad's daughter was born. She was only three when Grandad went into the army in 1941 to fight in the Second World War. He never came home from that war. But his daughter — Grandma's daughter — grew up, got married, and had a daughter of her own. Now Grandma is sharing her memories of her life with her granddaughter. What is the story of *your* Grandmother?